This book belongs to:

....

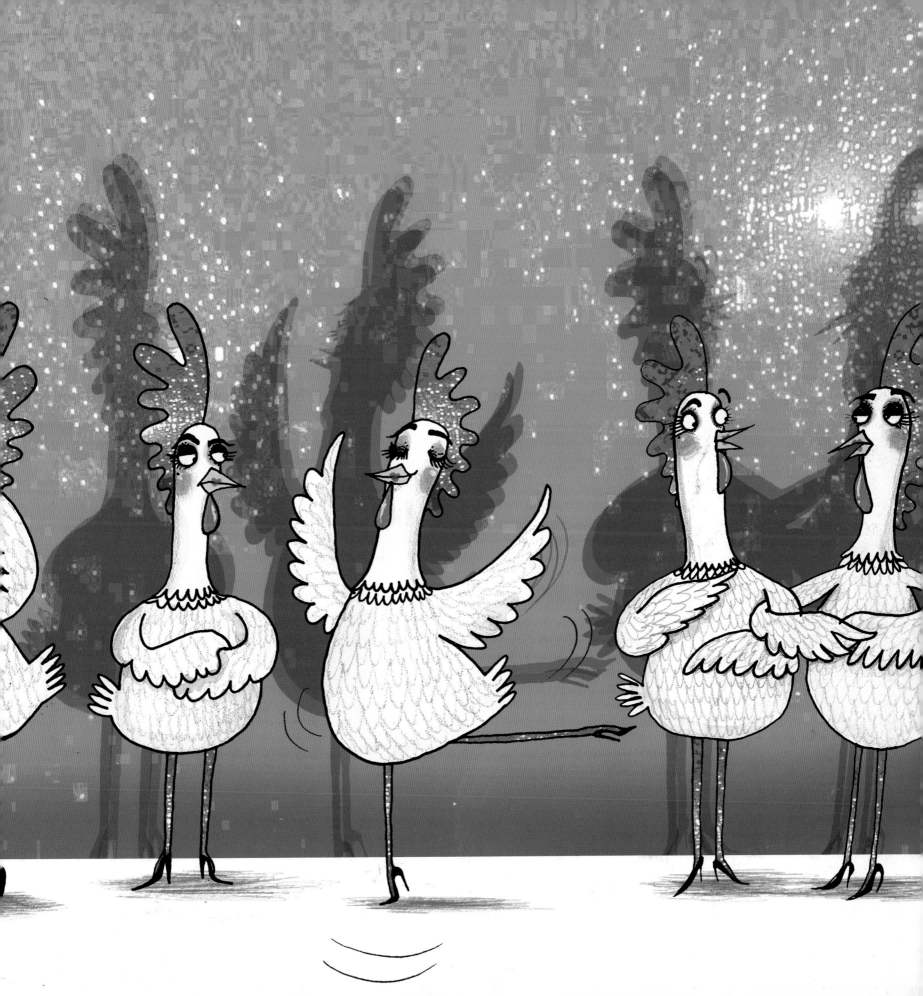

The author wishes to thank
MISS KATHRYN MILTON and MISS HOLLY SMITH,
and ALISON ELDRED for all her egg-cellent help.

Hodder *presents* EGG
Starring VIVIEN VIXEN *and* EDWARD L'OEUF
Co-starring MARLON BITEHARD
Directed by ALEX T. SMITH
Edited by EMMA LAYFIELD *Designed by* ALISON STILL

Chicken showgirls appear courtesy of *The Rosecomb Sisters*
'Shake Your Tail Feathers' Dance Troupe.

First released in hardback as *Egg* in 2010 by Hodder Children's Books
This paperback edition published in 2014
Text and illustrations copyright © Alex T. Smith 2010

Produced by Hodder Children's Books, 338 Euston Road, London, NW1 3BH.
In association with Hodder Children's Books Australia, Level 17/207 Kent Street, Sydney, NSW 2000.

ISBN: 978 1 444 92092 5
10 9 8 7 6 5 4 3 2 1

Hodder Children's Books is a division of Hachette Children's Books.
An Hachette UK Company. www.hachette.co.uk
A CO-PRODUCTION BETWEEN HACHETTE CHILDREN'S BOOKS
AND FOX AND HOUND PICTURES.

Foxy AND EGG

A book by
ALEX T. SMITH

Starring
VIVIEN VIXEN
as FOXY DuBOIS

Introducing
EDWARD L'OEUF
as EGG

Of all the suspicious looking
houses in all the deserted woods in
all the world, he had to roll up to hers...

Foxy DuBois was utterly charming
and always kind to strangers, so she
invited Egg in for a BITE to eat.

Whilst Foxy skipped off to the kitchen,
Egg rolled around the grand house.

'You have some interesting paintings,' shouted Egg.
But Foxy wasn't listening.

She was too busy cooking up a perfect cunning plan...

Chicken Pie

How to cook Eggs. • Boiled
Eggs make a • Fried
delicious treat • Scrambled.
for breakfast.

Foxy wanted
the biggest, most
delicious egg to eat
so she put part-one
of her sneaky plan
into action – she
would feed Egg up!

When dinner was
served it was a
very splendid affair.
Egg wobbled
with excitement.

Foxy wanted a big egg,
but she also wanted a
fit egg so, after dinner,
she put part-two
of her devious plan
into action – they
would play games!

They had
an egg-and-
spoon race
in the hallway,

played hide-
and-seek in
the library,

followed by
musical chairs in
the drawing room.

At the end of the night,
Egg was in a complete spin!
It had been a delightful
evening, but he needed to
rest his weary shell.

'You simply must stay over,'
said Foxy.
'I have something even more wonderful
planned for breakfast!'

As Egg snuggled
down in his cosy bed,
Foxy spent the night
dreaming eggy dreams...

There were
scrambled eggs
and fried eggs,
poached eggs
and baked eggs,
and, best of all,
soft-boiled eggs
and soldiers!

But when
Foxy DuBois
awoke the next
morning, she was
in for a shock…

During the night something had changed.
Egg was a fragile little thing no more. He was

ENORMOUS!

Foxy rubbed her hands with glee;
her crafty plan had worked.
It was going to be a big breakfast…

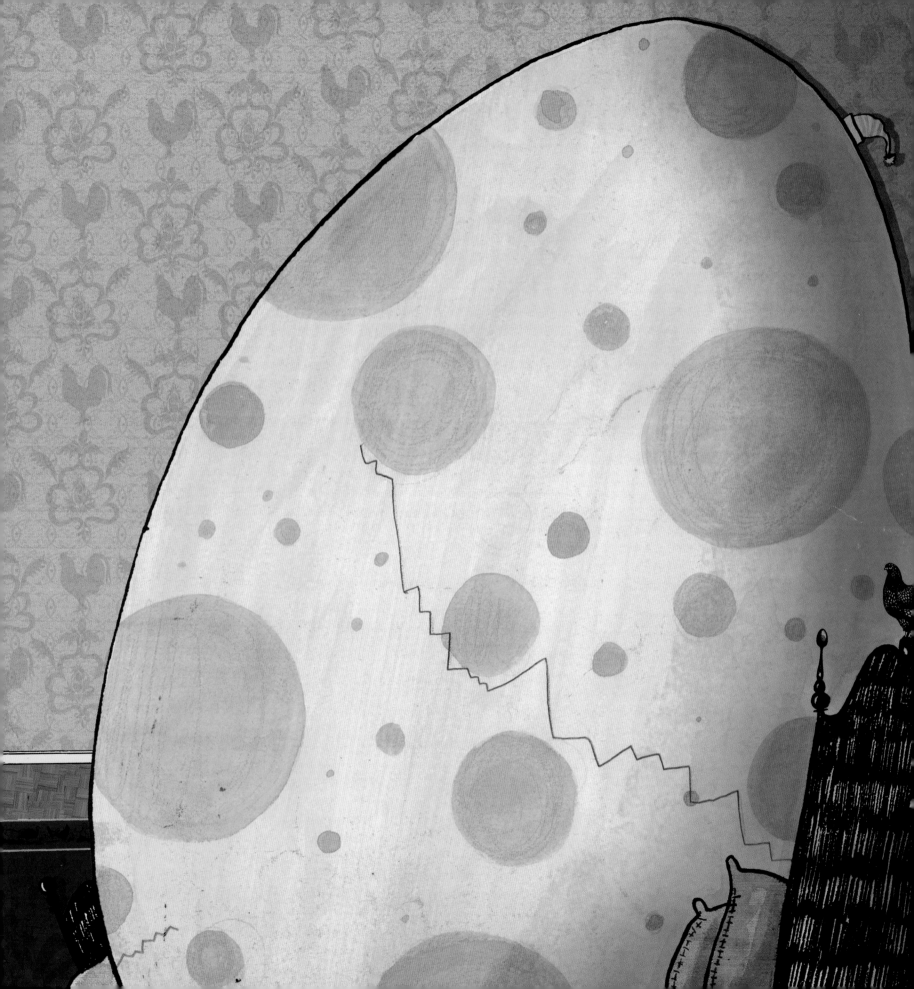

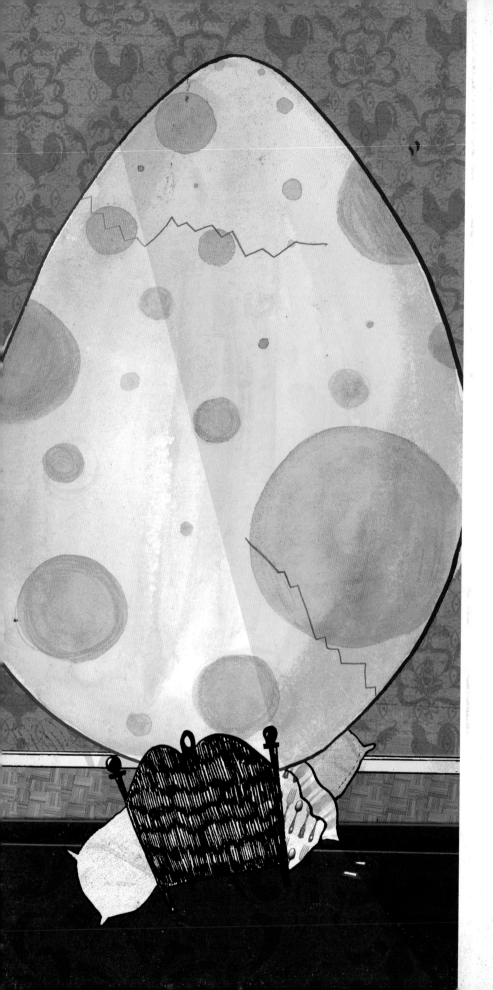

But just then Egg started to

CRACK!

Foxy licked her lips.

CRACK!

She licked her lips some more.
Then with one final crack,
Foxy saw what was inside...

'Good morning!'
said Alphonso wickedly.

'Am I in time for
breakfast?'

The End

Fabulous ALEX T. SMITH books:

Foxy AND EGG
978 1 444 92092 5

CLAUDE in the City
978 0 340 99899 1

CLAUDE on Holiday
978 0 340 99901 1

CLAUDE on the Slopes
978 1 444 90930 2

CLAUDE at the Circus
978 0 340 99903 5

CLAUDE in the Country
978 1 444 90928 9

CLAUDE in the Spotlight
978 1 444 90929 6

CATCH US IF YOU CAN-CAN
978 1 444 90366 9

FOXY TALES
978 1 444 90931 9

For fun activities, further information and to order, visit www.hodderchildrens.co.uk